Cute and Cuddly: Baby Animals

PUPPIES

By Grace Elora

Gareth Stevens Publishing

Please visit our Web site, www.garethstevens.com. For a free color catalog of all our high-quality books, call toll free 1-800-542-2595 or fax 1-877-542-2596.

Library of Congress Cataloging-in-Publication Data

Elora, Grace.
Puppies / Grace Elora.
p. cm. — (Cute and cuddly—baby animals)
ISBN 978-1-4339-4519-9 (library binding)
ISBN 978-1-4339-4520-5 (pbk.)
ISBN 978-1-4339-4521-2 (6-pack)
1. Puppies—Juvenile literature. I. Title.
SF426.5.E46 2011
636.7'07—dc22
2010038500

First Edition

Published in 2011 by
Gareth Stevens Publishing
111 East 14th Street, Suite 349
New York, NY 10003

Editor: Therese Shea
Designer: Andrea Davison-Bartolotta

Photo credits: Cover, pp. 1, 3, 5, 7, 9, 13, 15, 17, 19, 23, 24 (all) Shutterstock.com; p. 11 Javier Pierini/Getty Images; p. 21 Thinkstock.com;

Printed in the United States of America

CPSIA compliance information: Batch #CR118221GS: For further information contact Gareth Stevens, New York, New York at 1-800-542-2595.

PUPPIES

A baby dog is a puppy.

A mother dog can have many puppies.

A family of puppies is called a litter.

People must help feed a large litter.

Some puppies are big. Great Danes are big puppies.

Some puppies are little. Yorkies are little puppies.

Puppies go to the doctor. The doctor makes sure they are well.

Puppies sleep on each other. This helps them stay warm.

A puppy chews on toys.
It helps its teeth grow.

A puppy wags its tail when it is happy.

Words to Know

Great Dane

litter

wag

Yorkie